The *
Alonzo

Alonzo and Molly the Mermaid

Written by Debbie Kelly

This book is dedicated to my nephew William,
who inspired me to create Alonzo.

This book is designed to be dyslexia friendly.
For more information please visit www.bdadyslexia.org.uk

First published in paperback in Great Britain by Digital Leaf in 2012

ISBN: 978-1-909428-00-3

Text copyright © Debbie Kelly 2012
Illustrations copyright © Monika Filipina Trzpil 2012

Book printed in the EU.

Contents

Allow me to introduce Alonzo.

He is a chicken and, as chickens go,
he's quite cool. He loves his hat,
his music and having fun. He also has
some very special gadgets and knows
a little bit of magic. And because of
this, Alonzo always has adventures...

Chapter 1

Where's Molly?

It is a hot and sunny day and Alonzo wants to go underwater swimming, so he will need his magic scuba suit.

Alonzo loves swimming and sets off to his favourite beach. Last time he was here, he played hide and seek in the Rugged Reef with his friends.

So off he goes to the beach, gets ready and wades into the sea.

After a few minutes, he spots Alice the Angel Fish, who looks very upset.

'What's up, Alice? You don't look very happy.'

'Oh, Alonzo. I'm so pleased to see you,' she says as she bursts into tears. 'I really need your help.'

'What's wrong?' asks Alonzo.

'Well,' says Alice, 'we were all playing nicely in the underwater playground, when I turned round and noticed that Molly the Mermaid was missing! We can't find her anywhere!'

'Oh no,' says Alonzo, 'we need to start looking for her right away.'

So Alonzo and Alice swim off to join all the other sea creatures, to start hunting for Molly.

'Hello, everybody,' Alonzo says.
'It's lovely to see you all again. I was hoping we could all play hide and seek. Unfortunately, though, Molly has gone missing! I really need your help, please. We need to spread out and look in all the usual and unusual places. Can we meet back at the sparkly shells in 15 minutes?'

Chapter 2

Shell-shocked

Alonzo and Alice set off, looking everywhere they can think of. Is that Molly hiding behind the slimy seaweed? No. It's Sid the Squid.

'Have you seen Molly? We can't find her anywhere!' says Alice.

'No,' replies Sid. 'I've been here all morning and, until now, I haven't seen anyone.'

'Would you mind helping us try to find her? She's gone missing,' says Alonzo.

'Of course I will. I'll go and check the sunken ship; you know how much she loves hiding in it.'

'That's great,' says Alonzo. 'Thanks. We'll meet you back at the sparkly shells when you've checked.'

Alonzo and Alice swim off to the Rugged Reef and look in lots of possible hiding places. After a while they realise Molly is not there either.

'I think we should check the underwater playground once more, just to make sure Molly isn't playing a trick on us,' says Alonzo.

'OK,' replies Alice. 'But I really don't think Molly would do that. She knows I don't like having tricks played on me.'

Alonzo and Alice swim back to the underwater playground when suddenly, Alonzo gasps.

'Alice, do you remember seeing this oyster shell when you were playing here earlier?'

'No, I don't. How did that get there?'

Alonzo swims towards the shell, turns

his goggles onto x-ray mode, sees what is in the shell, and realises his worst fears are about to come true.

He swims down to open the shell, calling to Alice as he goes.

Alice helps Alonzo prise open the shell, where they find a note. Very slowly, trying not to let his voice shake, Alonzo starts to read...

'We have Molly the Mermaid. Give us 1,000 scoopernose fish and we'll release her. We need them to dig for treasure hidden under the seabed. Signed The Pesky Pirates.'

'Oh no,' wails Alice. 'Poor Molly. What should we do?'

'Right,' says Alonzo, 'we need a plan. Gather all the sea creatures together, from the smallest sea horse to the

biggest octopus. Ask them to meet me back at the squidgy seaweed when the tide turns.'

So off Alice swims, as fast as her little fins will go.

Chapter 3

A Clever Plan

When Alonzo finally arrives at the squidgy seaweed, there seems to be all sorts of sea creatures, ready to help the rescue mission. 'Marvellous,' he thinks. 'That's just what we need.'

'Hi, everyone. Thank you for coming together so quickly. You may have heard that the Pesky Pirates have kidnapped Molly the Mermaid. In return, they want 1,000 scoopernose fish to dig for treasure hidden under the seabed. We need to come up with a cunning plan to rescue Molly. And we need to tell all the scoopernose fish to hide. Those Pesky Pirates are very, very greedy.'

'The pirates' ship cannot be very far away, so can I ask all you strong, fast swimmers to search the seas and let me know if you find the ship, and if you can see Molly. Those of you who are smaller, swim as far as you can go and let me know what you see. Molly really needs us all to help her.'

A few minutes later, a group of sailfish return with the news that they have found the ship and have seen Molly sweeping the deck using her tail.

'Good work, you guys. Now we put the first part of the plan into action. I need the help of the dolphins,' says Alonzo.

'We're right here and ready to help,' says Delores the Dolphin.

'Great. This is what I was thinking: I need to get onto the ship, so I want you to put on a fabulous display of flipping, jumping and swimming to distract the Pesky Pirates long enough for me to get on and find a hiding place.'

'Easy enough,' says Delores. 'We'll go straight away.'

So off swims Delores and the rest of the dolphins to distract the pirates.

Alonzo waits until he hears shouts of delight, laughter and excitement from the ship. This is his moment!

As he sneaks onto the boat, he sees Molly sweeping the deck and sees, to his dismay, that the pirates have used a long chain and big lock to keep her there. She looks very unhappy and her tail isn't as shiny and colourful as normal.

He tiptoes over and taps her gently on the shoulder. She lets out a little

scream and turns around. Alonzo covers her mouth and asks her to be quiet and patient; he'll come back and rescue her soon. He needs to find the key for the big lock and he wants to teach the pirates a lesson.

Chapter 4

Pirate Punishment

Alonzo runs off to find a hiding place where the pirates won't find him. Eventually he finds a rusty-looking door which creaks when he opens it. Inside, there are some old buckets and spades, and lots and lots of spiders!

After taking off his magic scuba suit, Alonzo waits until he is sure it is night-time and the pirates have all gone to bed.

Quietly, he leaves the cupboard and creeps along the hall, stopping every now and then, listening for any noises from the pirates' bedrooms.

Very slowly, Alonzo opens a bedroom door. Fast asleep and gently snoring is a pirate called Atticus.

Alonzo mutters a few words under his breath and sprinkles some magic sand onto the pirate's face.

Atticus wriggles his nose, sneezes, and then rolls over, talking in his sleep.

'Ah ha! I'll get you and take all your treasure,' he says out loud.

Alonzo silently runs out of the bedroom, back to his hiding place, where he quickly falls fast asleep.

The next morning he is woken up by loud screaming. Alonzo knows exactly what has happened, and chuckles to himself.

Atticus has woken up and looked in the mirror, only to see that his nose has been turned into a scoopernose!

'Nnnnnnooooooo!!!!!' screams Atticus. 'Where's my nose?'

Alonzo giggles, puts on his magic scuba suit, runs from his hiding place and jumps overboard to go and tell all the sea creatures what he has done.

They all swim as fast as they can back to the ship to hear what the pirates are saying and doing. When they see what Alonzo has done, they can't help but laugh. Atticus looks very funny.

'Did he eat something strange last night?' asks one of the pirates.

'Do you think it's contagious?' asks another.

'We could use him instead of the scoopernose fish,' says the Captain.

'Nooo! How can we get my nose back?'

'I don't know,' says the Captain. 'Maybe we'll just have to wait and hope your normal nose will come back.'

'What if it doesn't?' asks Atticus.

The Captain doesn't reply.

'Have we heard anything from the sea creatures about them giving us our scoopernose fish?' asks the Captain.

'No,' reply the pirates.

'Right. Not only is the mermaid to sweep the deck using her tail, I want her to wash it as well!'

Chapter 5

More the Merrier

Poor Molly. Her tail is so tired. She knows that Alonzo will come back for her, but that doesn't stop the tears that gently slide down her face.

'Just be brave,' she tells herself.' Alonzo is clever and will have worked out a plan. Keep doing what the pirates ask and soon this will all be over.'

As the day draws to a close, Alonzo prepares to board the ship again.

When darkness falls, he creeps back onto the ship, finds Molly and tells her that he has a cunning plan. Molly finds it ever so funny and can't help but laugh out loud.

'Sssshhhh!!' says Alonzo. 'We don't want to wake them!'

Alonzo then runs off, back to his hiding place, where he takes off his scuba suit and gets ready to put his plan into action. Tonight, he must be really careful, as he is going to slip into each and every bedroom and use his magic sand again on all the pirates.

He starts on the lower deck of the ship, quietly entering the bedroom, casting the spell with his magic sand, and then silently closing the door behind him.

Alonzo quickly moves up to the next deck, turns the corner, and almost walks into the Captain!

Alonzo turns and runs back round the corner to hide, when he realises the Captain isn't following him.

'Didn't he see me?' thinks Alonzo.
He peeks around the corner, only to see
that the Captain is talking and walking
in his sleep!

'Phew. That was really close!'

After the Captain has walked by, Alonzo
continues on his way to the rest of the
bedrooms to cast his spell.

He leaves the Captain until last to make
sure he is tucked up in his bed after his
night-time walk.

Once he has cast his last spell, Alonzo
goes back to his hiding place again,
where he looks amongst all the buckets,
spades and spiders to find something soft
to rest his head on.

Finally, he finds a sponge inside the
smallest bucket, which he uses as a
pillow, and settles down for a quick snooze.

Chapter 6

Negotiating Noses

The next morning, the screams echo all around the ship and out to sea.

'What has happened to my face?'

'Where's my nose?'

'Aaaaaarrrghhhh!'

'Nnnnnoooooo!'

Suddenly, Alonzo jumps out of his hiding place.

'Ah ha, you Pesky Pirates. I did this to you for being so greedy and kidnapping Molly the Mermaid.'

'What do you mean, being greedy?' asks the Captain.

'I can't believe you don't know what I mean! You have sailed all over the sea and decided that you want the treasure that you think is buried under the sea bed.'

'You have become greedy. In your haste to gain more treasure you decided to capture Molly, chain her up and make her clean your ship, to try and force us to give you 1,000 scoopernose fish. You were then going to make those poor fish dig and dig for something that doesn't belong to you. How do you think that is right?' asks Alonzo.

The Captain looks really grumpy. He doesn't like being told anything other than he's pesky.

'Here's the deal. Firstly, you release Molly. Then you have a choice. You can stop being so greedy and I'll turn your noses back to normal, or you can continue being greedy, but you keep the scoopernoses and do the digging yourselves.'

The pirates murmur between themselves. They don't really want to give up having the scoopernose fish, which means no extra treasure, but they don't want these silly looking noses, either.

The Captain gathers the pirates round for a hushed talk.

'I have a plan. Let's tell Alonzo we're going to give Molly back, and that we realise how silly and greedy we've been, just so that he changes our noses back to normal. We'll pretend to argue about the treasure that we would have found. Make him think we've changed our ways. When the time is right, we'll try a different plan, one that won't fail. We are, after all, the Pesky Pirates!'

'Brilliant!' says Atticus. 'That sounds great. Do the rest of you agree?' he asks the other pirates.

'Yes. Let's do that,' they whisper, turning round to look at Alonzo with sly smiles.

Chapter 7

Free at Last!

Alonzo glares at the Pesky Pirates. They really are taking their time.

'I need you to release Molly right now.'

'OK, OK, here she is,' says the Captain, as he takes a gold chain from around his neck. It has the biggest key on it that Alonzo has ever seen. The Captain unlocks Molly from her chains.

Molly throws herself towards Alonzo, bends down and kisses him on his feathery face.

'Oh, Alonzo, thank you, thank you. My tail was getting so tired and sore from all that sweeping and cleaning.'

'I never thought I would get away. I have missed swimming and being with all my friends so much.'

'Right, Captain. Have you and your motley crew decided what to do about your noses?' asks Alonzo.

'What should we do?' asks Atticus.

'I wanted a ruby ring.'

'I wanted a gold watch.'

'I wanted to find a crown.'

'We want a load of gold coins!' bellow the pirates.

'Wait!' says the Captain as he winks knowingly at the group of pirates. 'This is ridiculous! I want, I want, I want! We have plenty of treasure at the moment, and there are plenty more islands for us to explore. Alonzo is right. We are being greedy. And I have to say, we all look particularly silly with these noses. Molly, I am sorry for chaining you up and making you work on our ship. And for our daft idea of using scoopernose fish.'

'Right, you pirates,' says Alonzo. 'If that's your decision, I need you to form an orderly queue and I will change your noses back to normal.'

Chapter 8

Forgive and Forget

One after another, Alonzo sprinkles magic sand onto the pirates' faces and with a quick twitch and a sneeze they turn back to normal.

'Oooooh,' says Atticus, 'that feels so much better.'

Alonzo looks at the pirates, and then to all the sea creatures. He leans towards them and whispers a question. He waits for their responses and turns back to the pirates.

'OK, I have one more question for you. Have you learnt your lesson?'

'Yes, yes we have, Alonzo. We are really, really sorry,' reply the pirates.

'Well, if that is the case, and you realise the error of your greedy ways, then I think it is about time we had some fun!'

And with that, Alonzo pulls on his magic scuba suit and jumps into the water with Molly to join all the turtles, fish and dolphins who are swimming around the ship.

'Jump in,' says Alonzo to the pirates as he bobs up and down in the sea.

'Are you sure?' asks the Captain. 'Aren't they still really cross with us?'

'Not at all,' says Alonzo. 'I asked them all whether we should let you join in and play, and they said as long as you were sorry, then that would be OK. They are fine. Come and have some fun with us.'

'Come on in and play,' calls Dolores.

So the pirates jump in.

The Captain looks around and sees Molly chatting to Alice. Leaving the rest of the pirates playing, he swims up to the two of them, stopping a little distance away, not wanting to interrupt.

Alice glares at the Captain, daring him to talk.

'Excuse me. Can I have a quick word with Molly?'

Alice looks at Molly to see whether that's OK. Molly nods her head.

'It's fine, Alice. I'm sure I'll be alright with the Captain now.'

Alice swims off to join Alonzo and Dolores, leaving Molly with the Captain.

'What about you, Molly? Do you forgive us?'

'Well, you were quite mean to me, and you made my tail very sore from all that cleaning.'

'PLEASE, Molly. PLEASE forgive us.'

'Oh, OK then, but you must promise that you'll never behave like that again.'

'I promise,' replies the Captain with his fingers crossed. 'Never again. And none of the other pirates will either. I think we have all learnt our lesson.'

'Oh, and there is just one thing you need to let me do,' says Molly with a smile.

'What's that?' he asks.

Molly gives him a great big grin, splashes water at his face with her tail, laughs and swims off, giggling as she goes. 'Catch me if you can!' is all he hears her yell.

The Captain watches her go, turns round to face the pirates and gives them a knowing smile and wink. 'Till next time...' he says.

The End

Spot the Difference

See if you can find all 8 differences
between these two very similar pictures.

Having trouble? Then contact the author for
help at www.facebook.com/alonzothechicken

Acknowledgements

There are many people who have encouraged and supported me to follow this dream of writing a book; too many to name here. However, there are some special and talented people who have to be mentioned.

Andrew, for his unfailing encouragement. My family, for their belief in me. Monika Filipina Trzpil, whose amazing illustrations have brought this book to life. Abbie Todd, whose critical editorial eye has reduced most of the mistakes; if there are any, they are all down to me. Ali Orchard who created Alonzo's Facebook page and finally, Digital Leaf, for having the confidence in Alonzo to bring him to life.

Debbie Kelly 2012